ATTACK OF THE PAPER BATS

BY MICHAEL DAHL
ILLUSTRATED BY MARTÍN BLANCO

Librarian Reviewer
Laurie K. Holland
Media Specialist (National Board Certified), Edina, MN
MA in Elementary Education, Minnesota State University, Mankato

Reading Consultant
Elizabeth Stedem
Educator/Consultant, Colorado Springs, CO
MA in Elementary Education, University of Denver, CO

STONE ARCH BOOKS
Minneapolis   San Diego

W9-BHV-095

Zone Books are published by Stone Arch Books,
151 Good Counsel Drive, P.O. Box 669,
Mankato, Minnesota 56002.
www.stonearchbooks.com

Library of Congress Cataloging-in-Publication Data
Dahl, Michael.
    Attack of the Paper Bats / by Michael Dahl; illustrated by
Martín Blanco.
    p. cm. — (Zone books - Library of Doom)
    Summary: When a mysterious wind blows the pages of a
book stolen long ago from the Library of Doom, it turns them
into sharp, bat-like objects that fly on their own, and only the
Librarian can stop them from attacking a young reader.
    ISBN-13: 978-1-59889-325-0 (library binding)
    ISBN-10: 1-59889-325-4 (library binding)
    ISBN-13: 978-1-59889-420-2 (paperback)
    ISBN-10: 1-59889-420-X (paperback)
    1. Books and reading—Fiction. 2. Librarians—Fiction.
3. Fantasy. I. Blanco, Martín, ill. II. Title.
PZ7.D15134Att 2007
[Fic]—dc22   2006027532

Art Director: Heather Kindseth
Cover Graphic Designer: Brann Garvey
Interior Graphic Designer: Kay Fraser

1 2 3 4 5 6 12 11 10 09 08 07

TABLE OF CONTENTS

The Library of Doom is the world's largest collection of strange and dangerous books. The Librarian's duty is to keep the books from falling into the hands of those who would use them for evil purposes.

CHAPTER 1

THE BOOK LEFT OPEN

A book lies open on the street.

The book belongs to the Library of Doom. It was stolen from the Library many years ago.

It traveled through many lands, passing from person to person.

The breath of a thousand readers mixed with the ink and sighed through the paper.

———◆———

After many years, a young boy saw the book in the window of a small store.

"That's the book I want," said the boy.

As the boy hurried home with his new purchase, the book fell out of his bag.

Now, the book lies in the street.
Its pages grow **warm** in the pale
moonlight.

CHAPTER 2

A STRANGE WIND

From out of nowhere, a cold wind blows down the street.

The wind shuffles the pages of the book. Several pages rip off.

The wind's invisible fingers fold and refold the pages into strange and deadly shapes.

The pages are sharp. The pages fly by themselves.

The pages are **hungry**.

On the **dark** street, the wind
rips off more pages.

CHAPTER 3

DARK WINDOWS

In another part of the dark city, the Librarian walks alone.

The wind **whistles** down
the street.

The Librarian pulls up his collar.
He lowers his head as he walks into
the wind.

As the Librarian stops in front of bookstores, he peers into the dark windows.

"None of these have the books I want," he whispers to himself.

The Librarian is searching
for books that were lost or stolen
from the Library of Doom.

A piece of paper flies overhead
in the wind.

A **scream** rips through
the dark.

〔 CHAPTER 4 〕

THE SCREAM

In another street, a young boy is reading a book.

He hears something scratch softly against his window.

The boy opens his window.

A small dark shape falls out of the sky.

"Ow!" yells the boy. A sharp piece of paper slashes his hand.

The boy tries to close the window, but the wind is too strong. More and more pieces of paper rush into his room.

They move as if they were not pieces of paper, but bats.

The boy **screams**.

21

CHAPTER 5

ATTACK!

The Librarian runs down a lonely alley.

He runs toward the sound of the scream.

Looking up, the Librarian sees
a cloud of pages.

Some of them are **flying** into
a small window high above him.

Somehow he must help the boy.

The Librarian leaps and grabs
the bottom of a fire escape. Quickly,
he darts up the metal stairway.

The Librarian crouches and then leaps. He flies across the alley.

As he leaps into the swarming ball of paper, the creatures attack.

He is surrounded.

The Librarian leans backward.
He loses his balance and **falls**
into the alley.

❲ CHAPTER 6 ❳

THE RIVER

The boy leans out his window.

He watches the paper bats leave his room and attack the man who tried to help him.

On the floor of the alley, the Librarian covers his head and face with his long, dark coat. Then he runs.

He cannot see where he is going, but he knows he cannot fight the swarm of pages.

The Librarian rushes down the alley. The alley drops off into a **dark** river.

The Librarian stops at the end
of the alley, and then dives.

The pages dive after him.

In the water, the pages lose their sharp edges. The paper **falls apart.**

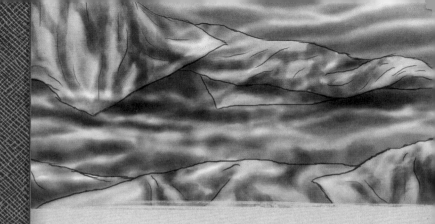

Everything sinks to the bottom
of the river.

In his room, the young boy looks
through the closed window.

Where is the **strange** man
who tried to rescue him?

THE END

A PAGE FROM THE LIBRARY OF DOOM

PAPER

The word "paper" comes from "papyrus," a plant that grew along the Nile river in Egypt. Ancient Egyptians peeled strips from the tall plants and pounded them flat to write on.

Ts'ai Lun, a member of the Chinese emperor's court in 105 A.D., is honored as the inventor of paper. He chopped up bamboo, bark from mulberry trees, and even fishing nets, to make a pulpy substance. When the pulp dried, it looked like our modern paper.

Today, paper is made from fibers that come mostly from trees, but can also come from straw or cotton.

Every year, the average student in the U.S. uses 700 pounds of paper!

Paper is dangerous! Brothers Homer and Langley Collyer never threw anything away. One day in 1947, they were found dead in their New York apartment buried under fallen stacks of old newspapers. It took rescuers 18 days to recover the bodies from beneath all the paper.

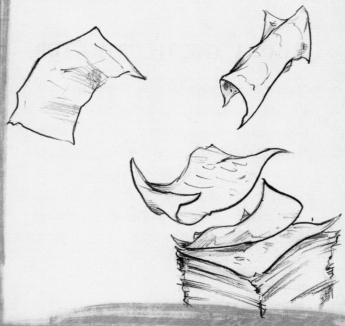

ABOUT THE AUTHOR

Michael Dahl is the author of more than 100 books for children and young adults. He has twice won the AEP Distinguished Achievement Award for his nonfiction. His Finnegan Zwake mystery series was chosen by the Agatha Awards to be among the five best mystery books for children in 2002 and 2003. He collects books on poison and graveyards, and lives in a haunted house in Minneapolis, Minnesota.

ABOUT THE ILLUSTRATOR

Martín Blanco was born in Argentina and studied drawing and painting at the Fine Arts University of Buenos Aires. He is currently a freelance illustrator and lives in Barcelona, Spain where he is working on films and comic books. Blanco loves to read, especially thrillers and horror. He also enjoys soccer, the Barcelona football team, and playing the drums with his friends.

GLOSSARY

dart (DART)—to move quickly

peer (PEER)—to stare, or look carefully

shuffle (SHUF-uhl)—to move something quickly from one place to another. A person might shuffle through the pages of a phone book, searching for a certain telephone number.

swarm (SWORM)—to move together in a big group. Sharks swarm; so do bees.

DISCUSSION QUESTIONS

1. At the begining of the story, a young boy buys the strange book that ends up in the street. Do you think the book landed in the street on purpose? Do you think the book knew what it was doing? Explain.

2. Why do you think the paper bats stopped attacking the boy and went after the Librarian instead?

3. What do you think happened to the Librarian after he dived into the river? What happened to the boy who was attacked?

WRITING PROMPTS

1. The paper bats all came from the same book, but we never learn what that book is about. What do you think? Use your own ideas and describe the kind of book it is. What is the book's title? What is it about? Does it have pictures? Would you want to read it?

2. What would the Librarian have done if there was no river nearby? How else could he have destroyed the swarm of paper bats? Write down another way he might have defeated them.

INTERNET SITES

Do you want to know more about subjects related to this book? Or are you interested in learning about other topics? Then check out FactHound, a fun, easy way to find Internet sites.

Our investigative staff has already sniffed out great sites for you!

Here's how to use FactHound:

1. Visit *www.facthound.com*

2. Select your grade level.

3. To learn more about subjects related to this book, type in the book's ISBN number: **159889420X**.

4. Click the **Fetch It** button.

FactHound will fetch the best Internet sites for you!